MW01013601

Absotively Posilutely

BEST EVIDENCE FOR CREATION

by Carl Kerby

Illustrated by Dan Lietha

Master Books®
A Division of New Leaf Publishing Group

Printed in the United States of America.

For information write: Master Books ® • P.O. Box 726 • Green Forest, AR 72638

Please visit our website for other great titles: www.masterbooks.net

ISBN 13: 978-0-89051-494-8

ISBN 10:   0-89051-494-1

Library of Congress Number: 2008935774

All illustrations within this book are by Dan Lietha except as noted:

    NASA: pages 14 & 15 (galaxies)
    NASA, ESA & H.E. Bond (StScl): page 15 (star)
    www.clipart.com: Page 21

Dedication

I want to dedicate this book to some dear friends who have had a major impact on my life.

First, of course, is Jesus Christ! Without Him there is nothing. The gift of salvation He gave me so many years ago is totally underserved. I pray that my life reflects well on His Word.

Second, my family! After salvation, you are the best gift that I've been given. The characters in this story are based on my children, Alisa and Dennis (aka Denny). My dear wife Masami is so important. Without her I'd be a mess. She keeps me humble! Thank you, Masami, for your patience and love throughout more than 25 years of marriage! I love you.

Ken Ham, for taking a chance on the son of a professional wrestler and air traffic controller. Not huge credentials to be involved in ministry! Thank you for looking beyond the exterior and allowing me to work with you these many years.

Miss Brenda Sue comes from two ladies names combined. (And I mean ladies. In our world today we don't have enough of them.) These two families have been an example to me on how to deal with tough times biblically! Thank you Rockwell's and Boone's for your godly example.

Dr. Jason Lisle and Dr. David Menton, who have the rare gift of being extremely intelligent, yet able to communicate to even the sons of wrestlers! Thank you both for sharing your wisdom. It is a privilege to work with you.

Last, but not least, Dr. John, (John in the story!). Thank you, sir, for your example and dedication, especially to prayer. I'll never forget watching you work with your patients. We need many more examples in our culture today of Christians sharing their faith in the marketplace. May God richly bless your service to Him.

"I can't wait to tell my friends!" yelled Denny. "This is fantastic!"

Miss Brenda Sue, the museum curator, watched as Denny ran out the doors of the museum. She had just shared with him the *best* evidence that God created the world and everything in it.

Racing across the field next to the museum, Denny saw his friend John.

"John, you gotta hear this. I just learned something amazing!" he said. "Do you know what the *best* evidence is that God created the universe?"

What Is Evidence?

Dictionary.com defines *evidence* as "that which tends to prove or disprove something; grounds for belief; proof." The way we understand evidence will be affected by what we believe about the past.

God tells us that His "word is true from the beginning" (Psalm 119:160)! What is comforting is that what we see in the world confirms what we read in God's Word!

4

"Hey, Denny," said John. "I think I know what the best evidence is! Just last night I was watching TV and saw an amazing show about giraffes. Did you know some giraffes have a heart that weighs almost 25 pounds and is two-and-a-half feet long?"

Denny was surprised. "No way! Why would their hearts be so big?"

"Because the dad giraffes can be almost 18 feet tall!" said John. "They need a big heart to pump the blood that high into the air. But a big heart isn't the only thing that makes them special. They also have one-way valves in the arteries going from their hearts to their brain!"

"One way valves? What're they for?" asked Denny.

"Well, if they didn't have them, there wouldn't be any giraffes!"

"Why's that?" asked Denny.

"It's kinda like this; remember the other day when we were playing leap frog?" asked John.

"Yep, what's that got to do with anything?" said Denny.

"You kept complaining about the headache you got from bending over for so long!" asked John.

"That's true!" exclaimed Denny. "My head hurt for almost an hour after we played."

A bull giraffe's heart can be up to 2.5 feet long and weigh over 20 pounds! That's a BIG heart.

- The skin of a giraffe is very tight, which helps force the blood out of the lower body back up to the heart. Without this skin, along with very small blood vessels in their lower bodies, the blood would stay in their legs causing them to swell!

- Giraffes have 32 teeth, just like most humans!

- Giraffes sleep only five minutes at a time for a total of 20 minutes of sleep per day! But, they spend up to 20 hours a day eating!

- Giraffes can run up to 35 mph.

- Giraffes can go months without drinking water, and when they finally do get a drink they can drink up to 12 gallons at a time!

- The giraffe's blood cells are 1/3 the size of a human's, allowing oxygen to be quickly moved throughout their bodies.

"You got the headache because gravity pulled the blood to your head as you bent over. Well, the same thing happens to a giraffe," John explained.

"If they didn't have the one-way valves in their arteries, giraffes would die whenever they bend over!"

"Oh, I get it!" said Denny. "Without the one-way valves, the blood from their big hearts would go straight into the giraffes' brains and kill them! That's a whole lot worse than my headache. But wait, when the blood hits that valve wouldn't the artery explode?"

"They talked about that too," said John. "Their arteries are flexible like a balloon. They swell up so they don't blow up!"

"Now that's cool!" said Denny.

"That's just a couple of things." said John. "I also learned that giraffes have seven neck bones just like us."

"Really?" said Denny "I would have thought they would have a lot more neck bones than us."

"Me too!" John said. "But they said if they had more neck bones than that there would be BIG problems. Right now it takes almost 500 pounds of muscles and tendons to make their necks work. If they had more neck bones, it would take more muscles and tendons, which would mean more weight. If giraffes had 14 neck bones their necks would be so heavy they'd fall over every time they tried to get a drink!"

"That'd be funny!" laughed Denny.

"Not for the giraffe. It just wouldn't work. So you see, Denny, only God could create something as amazing as the giraffe!"

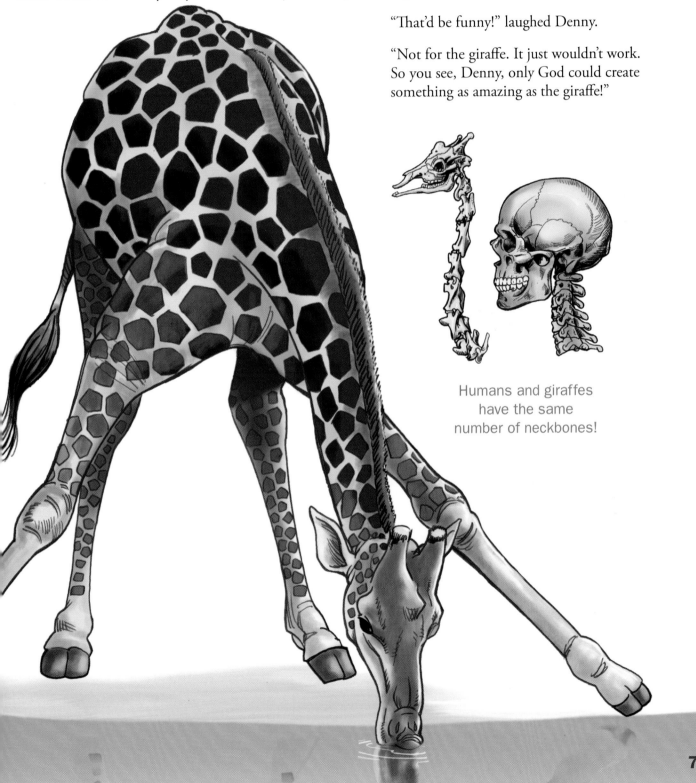

Humans and giraffes
have the same
number of neckbones!

7

"You're right, John, only God could create the giraffe. No way millions of years and chance could do all that, but it's not the *best* evidence that God created the universe," said Denny.

"It's not? What could be more amazing than a giraffe?" asked John. "Come on, I'll show you!" said Denny as he took off across the field.

A minute later they heard their friend Alisa calling to them from the edge of the woods. "Hey guys, where are you going? Let's play hide-n-seek!"

"Sorry Alisa, we can't stop now. We're going to see the *best* evidence that God created the universe," yelled Denny. "Maybe later!"

"Wait a second," Alisa called back. "I can show you the *best* evidence that God created the universe right over by the pond."

Frogs of Many Sizes!

• Frogs live on every continent except Antarctica! More than 60 percent of the Eastern Wood Frog's body can freeze during the winter and it will still survive.

• There are more than 4,700 species of frogs in the world.

• In certain environments some frogs secrete a painkiller that is 200 times more powerful than morphine and not addictive.

"Really?" said Denny coming to an abrupt stop. "That's great; let's go."

Off the three friends went with Alisa leading them down a path toward an amazing array of noises. As they got closer, they saw where the sound was coming from. It was a pond. Hundreds of tadpoles were swimming in the shallow areas busily searching for food.

"Here you go guys. Take a look at these tadpoles. They turn into one of my favorite amphibians," said Alisa.

"Frogs!" John and Denny called out in unison.

"You got it!" Alisa said. "I love frogs. Did you know there are more than four thousand different kinds of frogs? They're so different. It's hard to believe they're all frogs! Some frogs are so small you could put three adults on a nickel."

TADPOLE

EYE

TAIL

MOUTH

GILL

First They Swim, then They Hop!

The process of a frog developing from an egg is amazing. A frog starts from something that looks like a lump of jelly that grows a tail and external gills. Soon these gills turn into internal gills and the tail starts to disappear as the legs begin to grow. In the final stages of their development, the internal gills turn into lungs and the tail disappears completely, leaving the frog to hop through the rest of its life. All of this takes place in a matter of days.

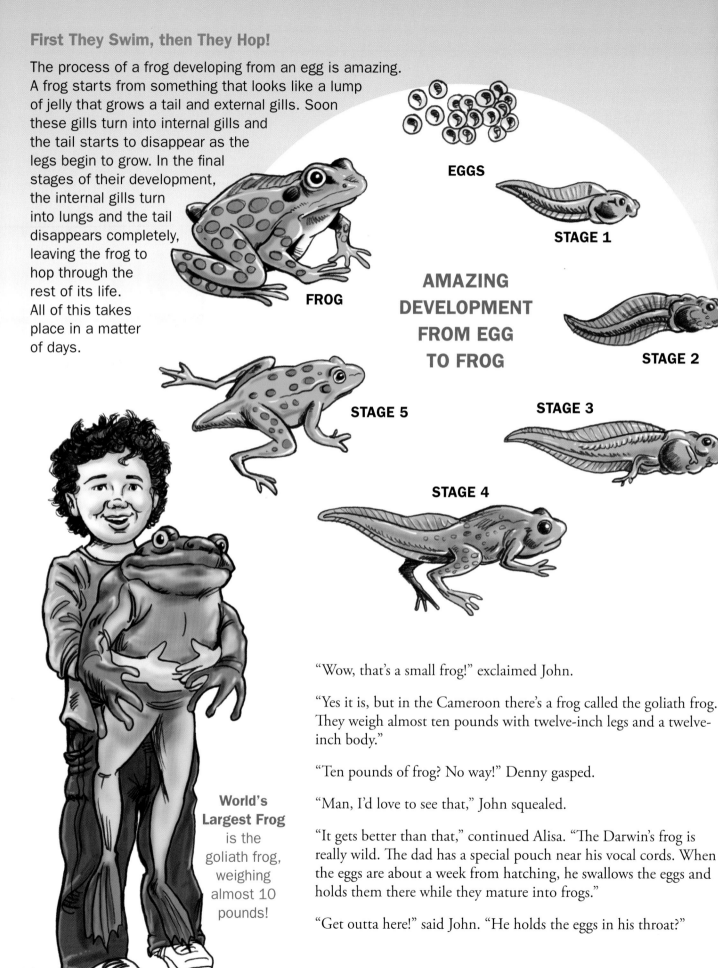

EGGS

STAGE 1

FROG

AMAZING DEVELOPMENT FROM EGG TO FROG

STAGE 2

STAGE 5

STAGE 3

STAGE 4

World's Largest Frog is the goliath frog, weighing almost 10 pounds!

"Wow, that's a small frog!" exclaimed John.

"Yes it is, but in the Cameroon there's a frog called the goliath frog. They weigh almost ten pounds with twelve-inch legs and a twelve-inch body."

"Ten pounds of frog? No way!" Denny gasped.

"Man, I'd love to see that," John squealed.

"It gets better than that," continued Alisa. "The Darwin's frog is really wild. The dad has a special pouch near his vocal cords. When the eggs are about a week from hatching, he swallows the eggs and holds them there while they mature into frogs."

"Get outta here!" said John. "He holds the eggs in his throat?"

10

"That's right, in a special pouch in his throat!" continued Alisa. "The eggs hatch, turn into tadpoles, then into frogs, all in that pouch. When the tadpoles have matured into a frog, the dad spits them out of his mouth!"

"No way!" Denny chipped in. "How did the dads figure out they had a pouch in their throats to put the eggs in? What did they do until they got the pouch?"

"Exactly!" Alisa said happily. "There is no way this could happen by tiny changes over a long period of time. It had to work the first time or there wouldn't be any Darwin's frogs. There are even more amazing frogs than this though!"

"What can be more amazing than that?" asked John.

"Well, there's the . . ." started Alisa.

"Wait a minute. Wait a minute!" interrupted Denny. "Alisa, I have to admit the frogs are way cool! I didn't know any of that. But, they aren't the *best* evidence that God created the universe. I've found something even better."

Got A Frog In Your Throat?

The eggs drop into the male frog's vocal sac, hatch there into tadpoles, and remain inside for another 50 to 70 days until they turn into froglets. During this time, the male's chest is puffed up with developing tadpoles.

World's Most Unusual Frog is the Darwin's frog. The daddy frog carries its eggs in its throat!

11

"Better than the frogs?" Alisa and John asked with puzzled looks on their faces.

"And better than the giraffe? Come on, I'll show you," Denny said as he took off running from the pond.

As they came around a bend on the path, they saw Maria.

"Where are you guys going in such a hurry?" called Maria.

Alisa answered excitedly, "Denny's taking us to see something really amazing!"

"Yeah, it's supposed to be cooler than frogs or giraffes," John continued.

"That's right!" Denny added. I'm going to show them the *best* evidence that God created the universe."

"Oh boy," exclaimed Maria. "I think I know what it is!"

They all stopped and looked at Maria, wondering what amazing example she would share.

"Awesome, that'll save us from any more running!" a tired John quipped.

"Yeah Maria, what is it?" Denny asked.

Maria said confidently, "That's easy! My dad and I were outside last night looking at the stars. He quoted a Bible verse to me that said: 'the heavens declare the glory of God.'"

Alisa spoke up, "The stars, of course! They are so beautiful."

"Yeah, and there are so many of them," added John. "I remember my dad reading a Bible verse to me that there are more stars than grains of sand on all the beaches and deserts on our planet!"

Denny tried cutting in, "But . . . !"

An excited Maria continued on. "Dad told me about that Bible verse. He said scientists studying the universe found something they couldn't believe."

This sparked Denny's interest. "What did they find Maria," he asked.

The Heavens Declare the Glory of God!

Each star gives off many different wavelengths of light. When we look at a star, we see the combination of all those wavelengths. That's what determines a star's color. By studying the array of different wavelengths of light, we can learn lots of interesting things about stars.

• The vast majority of stars are made up almost entirely of hydrogen and helium. Scientists can figure out what stars are made of by breaking down the light they emit into a "rainbow." By finding the colors that are missing from that "rainbow," they know what the star is made of! It's sort of like a fingerprint.

• Star colors also tell us how hot they are!

A. Blue stars, like Alnitak, which is one of three blue stars that make up Orion's belt, are very bright so they burn the hottest and quickest. These blue stars would have used all of their fuel a long time ago and not be visible if the universe were billions of years old. These blue stars support what the Bible teaches.

B. Yellow stars, like our sun, have a medium temperature. Aren't you glad that God knew what He was doing and placed a yellow star in our solar system? If it were a red or blue star, we wouldn't be here!! God is amazing.

C. Small, red stars, like Proxima Centauri, make up the majority of stars and have the coolest temperature. A very few red stars are big and bright. These are called "giants," or if they are really big, "supergiants." The bright star, Betelgeuse, is a red supergiant. If you see a red star at night, you can be sure it is a giant or supergiant. If it were not, it would be too faint to see.

• Stars come in types of clusters or bunches:

1. Open Clusters — made up of hundreds of stars.

2. Globular Clusters — made up of hundreds of thousands of stars.

• A galaxy like ours is made up of more than one hundred billion stars! Each galaxy would have many open clusters and globular clusters! Remember, we still cannot explain how a single star could happen all by itself, much less a galaxy!

• Stars come in different sizes. You would have to put 109 planets the size of earth side by side to get the width of the sun. That's nothing compared to the red supergiant Betelgeuse we talked about above. You would have to put 600 stars the size of our sun side-by-side to make up the width of Betelgeuse.

More than the Eye Can See!

When you look into the evening sky, the heavens truly declare the glory of God. Imagine a section of space the size of the period at the end of this sentence.

Within that tiny point in the sky, you could find multiple galaxies!

If you hold that period up to the night sky and imagine how much outer space is covered by it, you know just how small an area that is when compared to the rest of the sky.

In that small section of outer space, you would find 1,500 galaxies.

"Let me show you. Pick up a grain of sand." After they all had their piece of sand, Maria continued. "Hold the grain of sand in between two fingers and then hold your arm out straight. Imagine how much outer space is covered by that single grain of sand."

"O.K.! What's the point?" a confused Denny asked.

"Scientists took a picture of that much outer space. What they found amazed them! In that tiny section of space, they found more than one thousand galaxies," exclaimed Maria.

"More than one thousand galaxies under a grain of sand at arm's length?" gasped a shocked Alisa.

"They said you can take a picture in any direction, and you'll find the same thing!" said Maria. "Wow, that's a lot of galaxies!" said John.

Maria continued, "It's even more impressive than that. Dad told me the smallest galaxies are made up of millions of stars. The total number of stars that are visible using telescopes is 70,000,000,000,000,000,000,000 (70 sextillion)!"

"That's a huge number. I didn't know anyone could even count that high!" said Denny.

"Remember, that's just the stars we can see," continued Maria. "One scientist said the number of all stars in the universe, including the ones we can't see, could be infinite!"

Wagging his head, an overwhelmed John said, "That's a huge number! Why isn't that the best evidence that God created the universe?"

"What I love is how beautifully designed the stars and galaxies are," said Maria. "A single star is so complex that no one knows how it could form all by itself! There are billions and billions and billions of stars! How could they form without God doing it? They have to be the *best* evidence that God created the universe!"

Each galaxy is made up of millions of stars. Many galaxies contain more than 100 billion stars!
Fun Fact: There are 1 billion galaxies inside the cup of the Big Dipper alone.

"Hold on guys!" said Denny. "The stars are fantastic, no doubt about it. If Miss Brenda Sue hadn't talked with me earlier, I would have said they're the *best* evidence. But, there is something that is even better than the stars."

A puzzled Alisa looked at John and Maria. "Wait a second, Denny. We're going to work this out." Alisa, John, and Maria huddled together, excitedly making suggestions about what the *best* evidence for creation might be. Denny listened as they talked back and forth.

"What about birds? They're pretty amazing," said one. "Yes they are, but what about us? Our bodies are pretty cool," said another. Finally, after a few minutes, he heard them say, "If it isn't the stars, frogs, or giraffes, what could it be???"

An excited John clicked his fingers and shouted, "I've got it! It's the dinosaurs!"

"Yeah," agreed Alisa and Maria. "They were amazing. It has to be the dinosaurs!"

"My favorite dinosaur is the T-Rex, and . . ." started John.

"Sorry guys!" Denny called out. "That is exactly what I thought when Miss Brenda Sue asked me what I thought was the *best* evidence. We talked about dinosaurs for a long time. They were amazing. You may not believe me now, but there's something even more incredible. Come on, I'll show you."

By now John, Alisa, and Maria had no idea what to expect. All they knew was they wanted to know the answer. Racing across the field, they returned to the museum, where Denny had been earlier that morning.

As they walked into the door, they saw Miss Brenda Sue. Denny called to her, "Miss Brenda Sue! I brought some of my friends with me, and they want to see the *best* evidence that God created the universe."

Miss Brenda Sue looked over at the four young friends with surprise. "Wow! That was quick!"

"Denny told us you've got something more amazing than frogs, stars, or even giraffes. Please tell us what it is!" John, Alisa, and Maria said.

"You bet I will! Good job Denny," said Miss Brenda Sue. "Getting others excited about our world is a wonderful way to share the *best* evidence with folks. Why don't we show them together Denny?"

"Can I?" shouted Denny.

"You bet. Let's go!" said Miss Brenda Sue.

"Finally, we can't wait!" cheered John, Alisa, and Maria.

Amazing Facts about Dinosaurs!

• The word dinosaur means terrible lizard. Sir Richard Owen coined the name in 1842.

• We know dinosaurs existed because we find their bones. These bones are called fossils.

• Dinosaurs stood erect with their legs beneath them like a cow, instead of like a modern-day reptile's legs, which sprawl to the side.

• The largest dinosaurs were more than 100 feet long and up to 50 feet tall. This is still smaller than a blue whale, which can be up to 110 feet long.

• The smallest dinosaurs were about the size of a chicken.

• Some Triceratops were as long as a bus, and the Brachiosaurus could be as long as a tennis court!

• There are two types of dinosaurs. They are bird-hipped (ornithischians) and lizard-hipped (saurischians).

• Recently a T-rex bone was found that contained what appears to be soft tissue. The same fossil had blood vessels that were still flexible and contained blood cells, bone matrix, and connective tissue, supporting a younger earth as taught by the Bible.

• The first dinosaur to be officially described was the Megalosaurus. It was found in England in 1677.

Off they walked until they got in front of a display showing two men working at a dinosaur dig site.

"OK, Denny, why don't you start us off?" asked Miss Brenda Sue.

"All right, guys," Denny called out as he hopped around excitedly. "This area really helped me understand what the *best* evidence is. Both of these guys are scientists. But one is a Christian, and the other one isn't. They're both looking at the same evidence. The problem between Christians and non-Christians isn't the evidence. We've all got the same evidence. The problem is how we interpret the evidence."

"I don't understand!" said Alisa.

"It's like this Alisa. You wear glasses, right?" asked Denny.

"I sure do." Alisa responded.

"Well, if you take off your glasses, do things look different?" asked Denny.

"That's for sure. Without them everything is blurry." laughed Alisa.

"Well the same is true when we look at the world," explained Denny. "The Bible is like a pair of glasses that we look through to understand the world. As a Christian, we have been given a history from the only One who has always been there — God!

So when we look at the world with the Bible as our starting point, we understand everything differently. The Bible makes blurry things and makes them clear!"

"Excellent, Denny!" said Miss Brenda Sue. "It's very important to understand that EVERYONE looks at the world through a pair of glasses. Those glasses are called a "worldview." People who don't believe the Bible have the same evidence we have, they just understand it differently because of their worldview."

"OK! That makes sense. What's that got to do with the *best* evidence that God created the universe?" asked Maria.

"Well, remember the glasses illustration and think about this. Who's the only One that knows everything?" asked Miss Brenda Sue.

"That's easy, God!" all three exclaimed in unison.

"Right!" continued Miss Brenda Sue. "Who's the only One who's always been there?"

"God of course," the three piped up.

Denny then joined in, "Right again! How do we know what God did in the past?" he asked.

NON-CHRISTIAN WORLDVIEW

- The present is the key to the past.
- Hydrogen gas balled itself together to become a star.
- Feathers evolve from scales.
- Unguided material processes produce man.
- Man is nothing special.

CHRISTIAN WORLDVIEW

- Revelation is the key to the past.
- God spoke the stars into existence on day four of creation.
- God created the feather when He created the first bird on day five of creation.
- God formed man on day six of creation.
- Man is created in the image of God.

- When we die, that's all there is.

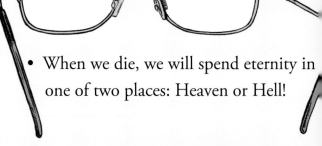

- When we die, we will spend eternity in one of two places: Heaven or Hell!

Thinking carefully about her words as she spoke, Alisa said, "Well, the Bible tells us what happened."

"Now I get it!" said Maria excitedly.

"What is it?" asked John.

Maria continued. "If God is the only One who knows everything, and He told us what happened in the Bible, that means the *best* evidence that God created the universe is the Bible. That's where He told us that He created everything!"

"I see!" said Alisa. "That makes sense. This means the Bible's not a storybook. It's actually a history book given to us by the only One who knows everything and was always there!"

"Excellent, Alisa," said Miss Brenda Sue. "What's even more amazing is that God not only told us He created, but He also told us when, what, and how He created! People who don't believe in God will try to confuse you about this. Many times they will say that you can't trust the Bible because it was just written by men and it is old and outdated."

"I've had friends tell me that before," answered Maria. "They said they heard it on TV!"

"It's unfortunate, but true, that many times TV and movies teach a history different from what the Bible teaches, and this confuses people," said Miss Brenda Sue. "If you watch these shows, pay attention to what is being said and compare it with what God says. Remember, God knows more than people do!"

"OK," said John. "Let me see if I understand. Christians and non-Christians explain what we see in the world differently because of the glasses they are wearing. Non-Christians see the world as if millions of years is what made it happen. Christians see the world as if God made it happen!"

Amazing Facts about the Bible!

• The Bible is made up of 66 books written by approximately 40 authors, who were from all walks of life, including fishermen to doctors, over about 1,500 years.

• In A.D. 1238, Cardinal Hugo de S. Caro separated the Bible into chapters. As a result, there are now 1,189 chapters in the Bible.

• In 1551, when printing became possible, Robertus Stephanus broke the Scriptures into verses. Now there are 31,101 verses made up of more than 770,000 words.

• The Bible was originally written in three different languages — Hebrew, Aramaic, and Greek. It has now been translated into more than 1,200 different languages.

• Contained in the 783,137 words of the Scriptures there are 1,260 promises and more than 8,000 predictions. In addition, there are more than 3,100 fulfilled prophecies. No other book can make such a claim.

• According to various sources in the United States, there are about 168,000 new Bibles sold, given away, or otherwise distributed daily. I pray you are studying God's Word and gaining knowledge to share with those who don't know Jesus as Savior.

"Absolutely right!" exclaimed Miss Brenda Sue. "Now what you need to do is study the Bible, learn what it teaches, and then look at the world we live in to understand it. We don't use evidence to prove the Bible because evidence is understood by what we believe about the past. What we see in the world does fit with what God's Word says though. It doesn't contradict the Bible at all."

"The thing that I really remembered from our first meeting," chipped in Denny, "is that as a Christian we have to choose who we're going to trust! We can trust God and His Word because it is real history, or we can trust man's opinion that changes every time a new rock is found somewhere."

"Absolutely!" said Miss Brenda Sue. "The Bible tells us to choose who we're going to follow and that the Bible is true 'from the beginning.' And that's why it is the *best* evidence that God created the universe!"

"All right, we get it!" said John, Maria, and Alisa. "Thanks a lot. We've gotta go tell our friends! See you soon. Bye!" With that they ran to share what they had learned.

May God richly bless and encourage you today. Love God enough to share your faith with someone you meet today, and pray for those who don't know God as their Creator, Redeemer, and Savior.

Amazing Facts about the Christian Faith!

There is no doubt that the Bible absotively, osilutely is trustworthy and true! What we see in the world confirms this. That's because the Bible is real history, and it has been given to us from the only one who has always been there and knows everything — God!

There is a very sad account in the Bible about the rebellion of the first man, Adam, against God's command. This brought death, suffering, and separation from God into this world. We see the results all around us. Even though there is beauty and design in the amazing animals we talked about, we also see many ugly things as a consequence of our rebellion.

• All of Adam's descendants, you and I, are sinful from birth (Psalm 51:5). Because of this, we cannot live with a holy God but are condemned to separation from God.

• The Bible says that "all have sinned and fall short of the glory of God" (Romans 3:23) and that all are therefore subject to "everlasting destruction from the presence of the Lord and from the glory of His power" (2 Thessalonians 1:9).

• The good news is that God has done something about it. "God so loved the world that He gave His only begotten Son, that whoever believes in Him should not perish, but have everlasting life" (John 3:16). Imagine that, the Creator of all that we see, though totally sinless, suffered on our behalf. Because of our sin, He paid the price of death and separation from God.

• Therefore, "He who believes in Him is not condemned; but he who does not believe is condemned already, because he has not believed in the name of the only begotten Son of God" (John 3:18).

• We have a wonderful Savior, who is also our Creator. His name is Jesus Christ, and He is the way, the truth, and the light. No one comes to the Father except by Him (John 14:6). Please trust Him today, His creation leaves no doubt that He's there. His Word leaves no doubt that He loves you!

A FIELD TRIP IN A BOOK

An unforgettable learning adventure through the Creation Museum. See history unfold before your very eyes . . . perfect for all ages!

8 x 8 • 160 pages • Spiral Casebound • Color interior • $18.99 • ISBN-13: 978-0-089051-538-9

The Complete Creation Museum Adventure takes you on an exciting exploration of God's Word as you journey through biblical history. Unearth biblical truths and amazing facts about dinosaurs, the Garden of Eden, Noah's ark, fossils, and much more! Travel along with young detectives Cody and Kayla as they search for answers to important questions about the Bible and the world around them. Uncover the tools you need to prepare for your informative journey, enjoy an awesome walk-through-the-museum experience, and reinforce learning with fun activities for the whole family. Truly an exciting experience like no other!

CREATION MUSEUM
Prepare to believe.

For more information about the museum, please visit: www.creationmuseum.org

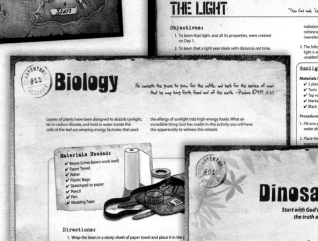

Available at your local Christian bookstore or call 1-800-999-3777

Includes these great extras:

- Adventure Map
- 7 Cs Timeline Bookmark
- Fact Finder Cards
- Creature Feature Cards
- Eyewitness Cards
- Challenge Cards
- Case Files/Devotionals
- Teacher Guides
- Reproducible Activity Sheets